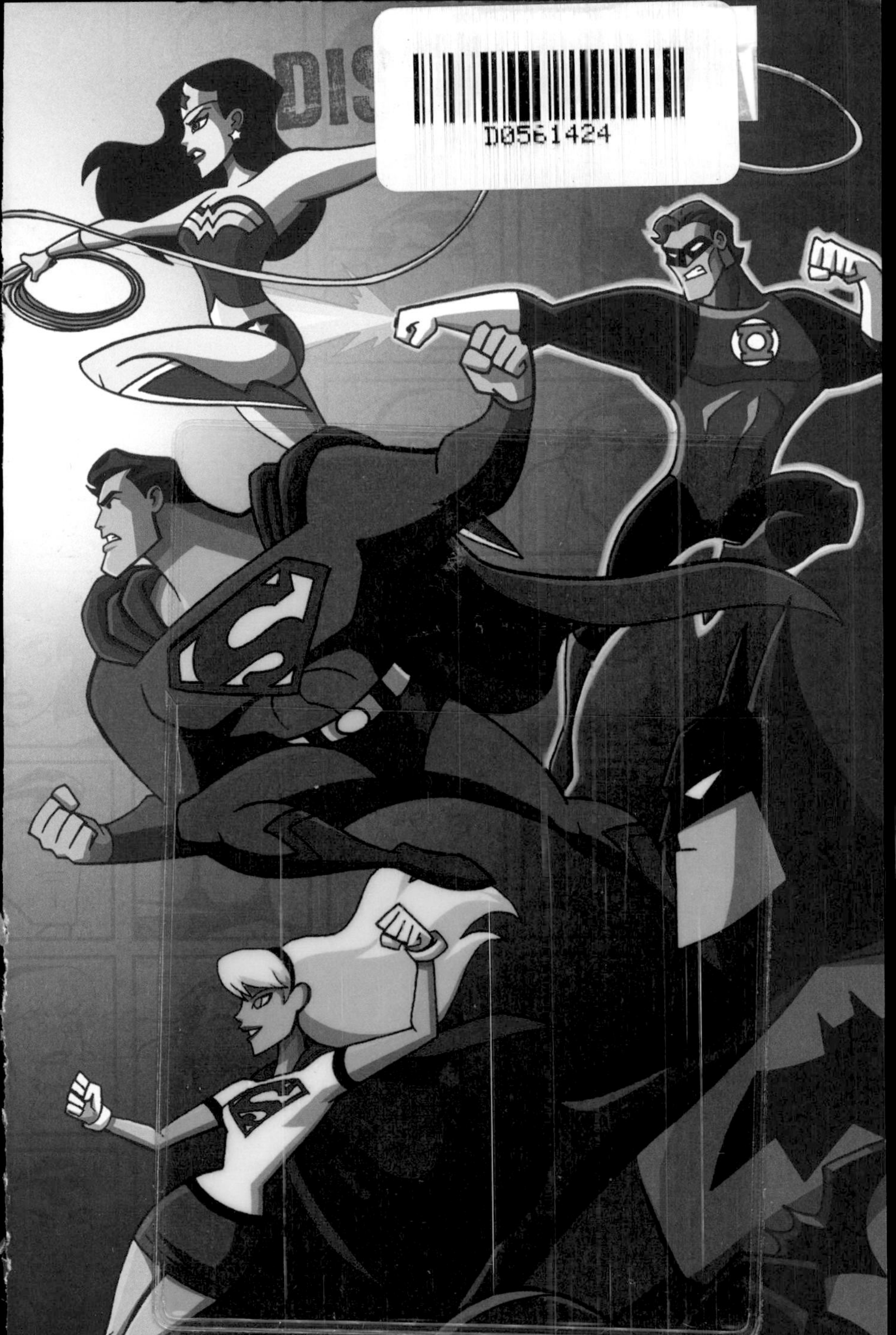

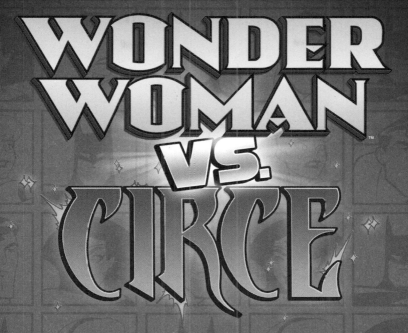

WONDER WOMAN™ VS. CIRCE

WRITTEN BY
LAURIE S. SUTTON

ILLUSTRATED BY
LUCIANO VECCHIO

WONDER WOMAN CREATED BY
WILLIAM MOULTON MARSTON

STONE ARCH BOOKS
a capstone imprint

Published by Stone Arch Books in 2013
A Capstone Imprint
1710 Roe Crest Drive
North Mankato, MN 56003
www.capstonepub.com

STAR29362

Cataloging-in-Publication Data is
available at the Library of Congress website.

ISBN: 978-1-4342-6014-7 (library binding)

Summary: Circe the super-sorceress has managed to
get her hands on three ancient fragments imprisoning
a mythical monster. When Circe unleashes the mystical
beast, it overpowers her mind — and steals her powers!
Only Wonder Woman can stand up to their combined
strength and save her mortal enemy — and the world —
from certain doom.

Designed by Hilary Wacholz

Printed in the United States of America in Stevens Point, Wisconsin.
032013   007227WZF13

TABLE OF CONTENTS

WONDER WOMAN™

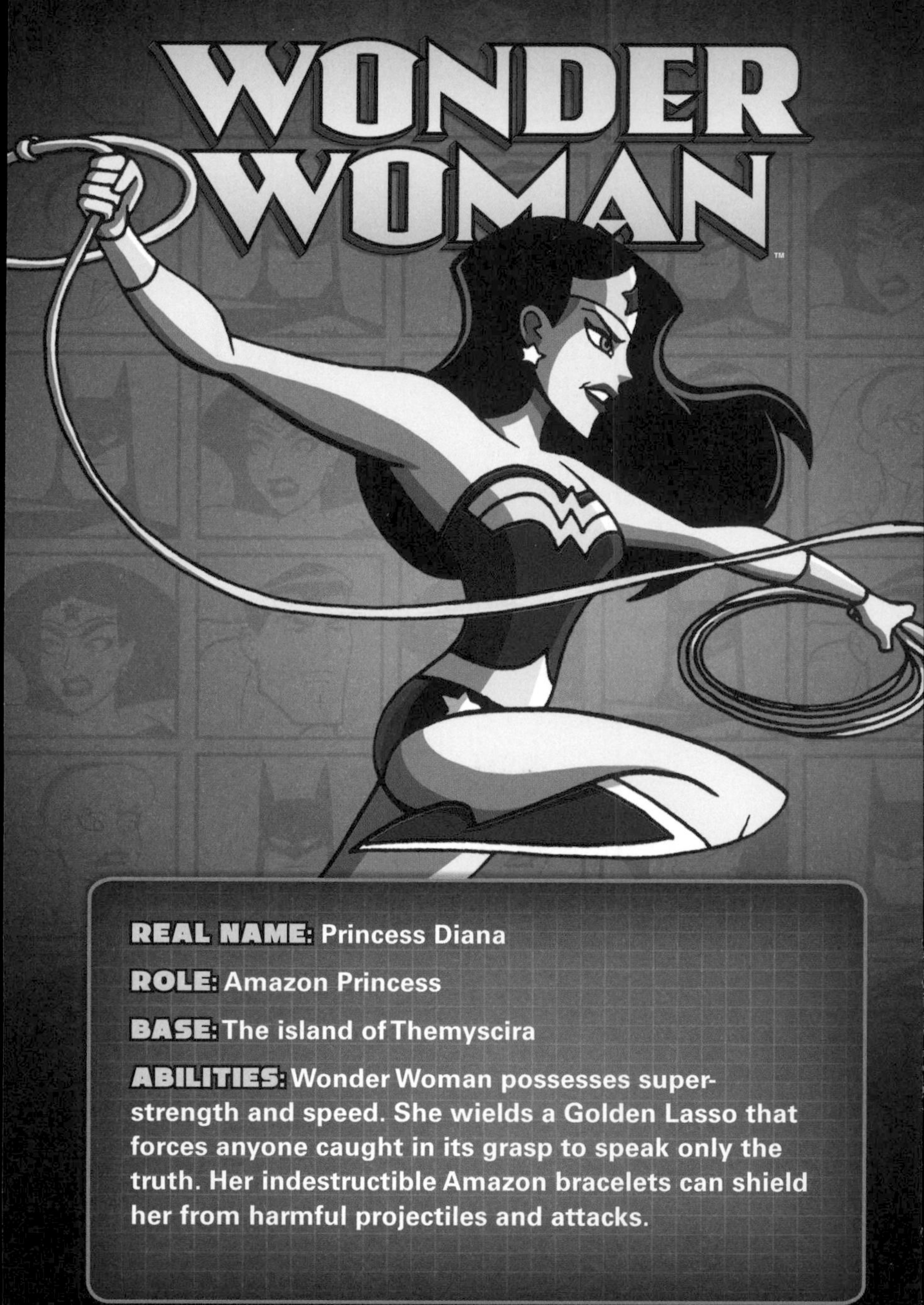

REAL NAME: Princess Diana

ROLE: Amazon Princess

BASE: The island of Themyscira

ABILITIES: Wonder Woman possesses super-strength and speed. She wields a Golden Lasso that forces anyone caught in its grasp to speak only the truth. Her indestructible Amazon bracelets can shield her from harmful projectiles and attacks.

CIRCE

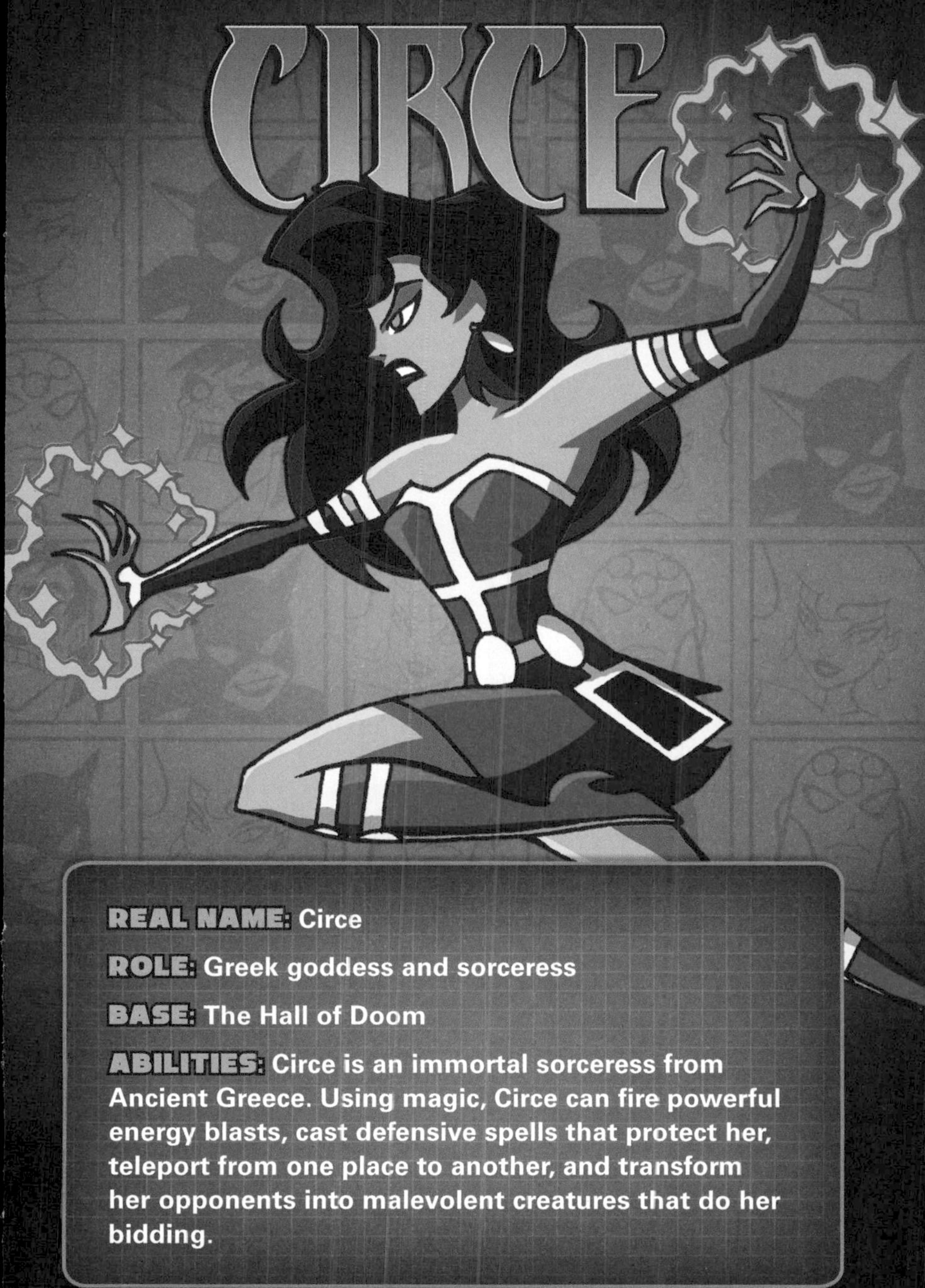

REAL NAME: Circe

ROLE: Greek goddess and sorceress

BASE: The Hall of Doom

ABILITIES: Circe is an immortal sorceress from Ancient Greece. Using magic, Circe can fire powerful energy blasts, cast defensive spells that protect her, teleport from one place to another, and transform her opponents into malevolent creatures that do her bidding.

CHAPTER 1

THE BOX

Circe, the immortal sorceress, chanted a powerful spell. "In darkest night, let shadow's might, with mighty force, bring chaos forth!"

A strange brew bubbled in a stone pot despite there being no fire beneath it. A circle of thirteen candles surrounded the pot. They emitted a pale, sickly light. Circe tossed a pinch of mystic powder into the cauldron. **FWOOOOOSH!** Tendrils of flame and scarlet light twisted into the air.

"Powers of flame and thunder," Circe chanted, "destroy the woman of wonder!"

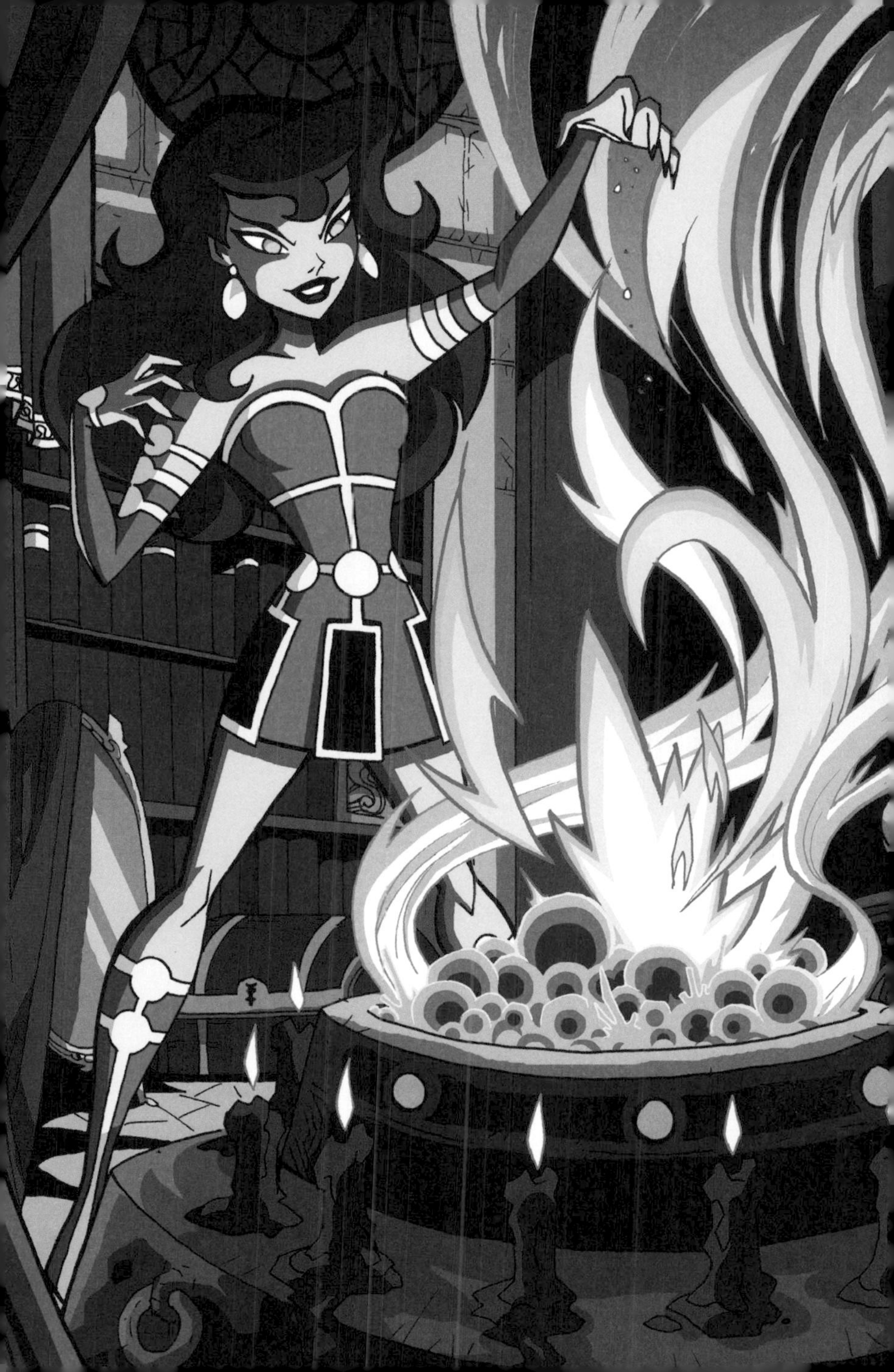

Circe was nearly shouting now. Her hatred of Wonder Woman was fueling the spell. Her emotions became as intense as the blaze, which made the flames grow even stronger.

KABOOOOM! The spell exploded in a puff of smoke. "Curses!" Circe exclaimed. "This is the third time in a row my spell has failed."

She stepped away from her cauldron and walked toward a wall of shelves. It was filled with books of all shapes and sizes. Every spell the sorceress had collected over the centuries was in this library. It held a vast amount of magical knowledge . . . but not a single spell that could destroy her archenemy, Wonder Woman.

SCRATCH! SCRATCH!

SCRATCH! SCRATCH!

Strange sounds suddenly came from a long-forgotten mirror in a corner. A mirror Circe hadn't thought about for many, many years. At first she did not even remember what was concealed there.

"At last! In my hands . . . the great power!" a voice hissed from the dark corner.

Circe's eyes went wide. Memories hit her like a tidal wave. She had recently cast a spell on a certain artifact. And the spell had worked — just not on the target she'd expected.

Circe ran toward the whispering voice from the magical mirror. ". . . all the evils of the world . . . ," the voice whispered.

Circe grabbed the mirror with both hands. Images moved across its surface. The sorceress could see a man wearing dusty clothes.

Circe saw that the man was holding up a clay container. "That box emanates magical powers," Circe said, sensing its strength. "It will be mine!"

Circe spoke a teleportation spell. POOOOF! She disappeared in the blink of an eye and instantly reappeared in a dark tomb. A man was kneeling on the ground in front of Circe. He held the clay box in his hands, almost dropping it when he saw her.

"I'll take that," the sorceress said. She lifted the artifact from his shaky grip.

"You're . . . ," the man stammered.

"Circe," the sorceress confirmed. "You know who I am. But who are you?" Circe looked into the man's eyes. Her powers let her see his entire life in mere moments.

"You are Dr. Leo Roberts," she said. "A tomb raider."

"Yes, I am," he said guiltily.

The sorceress held up the artifact. It looked like an ordinary clay container, but Circe recognized it immediately.

"You have found Pandora's Box! I've been looking for this for thousands of years!" she declared, grinning at the man. "You have served me well in this task. Now you will serve me forever."

The sorceress lifted a hand, starting a spell that would turn him into one of her slave creatures. The tomb raider raised his arms to shield his body.

"Please spare me!" he blurted. "If you do, I'll tell you where the Trinity Beast is hidden!"

Circe stopped her spell in the middle of a syllable. Sparks jumped from her fingers and drifted down, vanishing in the dirt.

"The Trinity Beast?" she repeated. "The combination of the forms and powers of the Hydra, Griffin, and Gorgon?" Circe laughed at his boast. "How can a mortal like you know where it is? The original statue of the Beast was broken into three pieces and scattered across the Earth."

"It is my business to know," the tomb raider said. "I make a lot of money finding ancient things."

Circe knew the man's reputation. He went to risky lengths to get the goods.

"That's why I was looking for Pandora's Box," he explained. "It's the only thing that can safely hold the Beast."

This made sense to Circe. Pandora's Box had the strength to hold all the evils of the world — until Pandora opened it. It could contain the power of the Trinity Beast.

"Very well, Dr. Roberts," Circe said. "Tell me where to find the Trinity Beast, and I will spare your life."

The tomb raider almost sobbed. "I only know where one fragment is," he confessed.

Circe held down her anger. She wanted the whole Beast for one reason: with it, she could destroy Wonder Woman!

"One piece will lead you to the others," Dr. Roberts said. "The three fragments are connected. Find one, and it will lead you to the rest."

"Tell me where the first fragment is!" Circe demanded.

"It's hidden in fire," the tomb raider said. "It's buried in Mt. Vesuvius."

"A volcano?" Circe grumbled. "That must be the work of Hephaestus, the god of fire and the forge."

The sorceress waved her hand and completed her spell. **POOF!** Dr. Roberts transformed into the combination of a lion and a bird. He flapped his wings in surprise and roared.

"What are you complaining about?" Circe asked. "I promised to spare your life. I never said you'd spend the rest of it as a human."

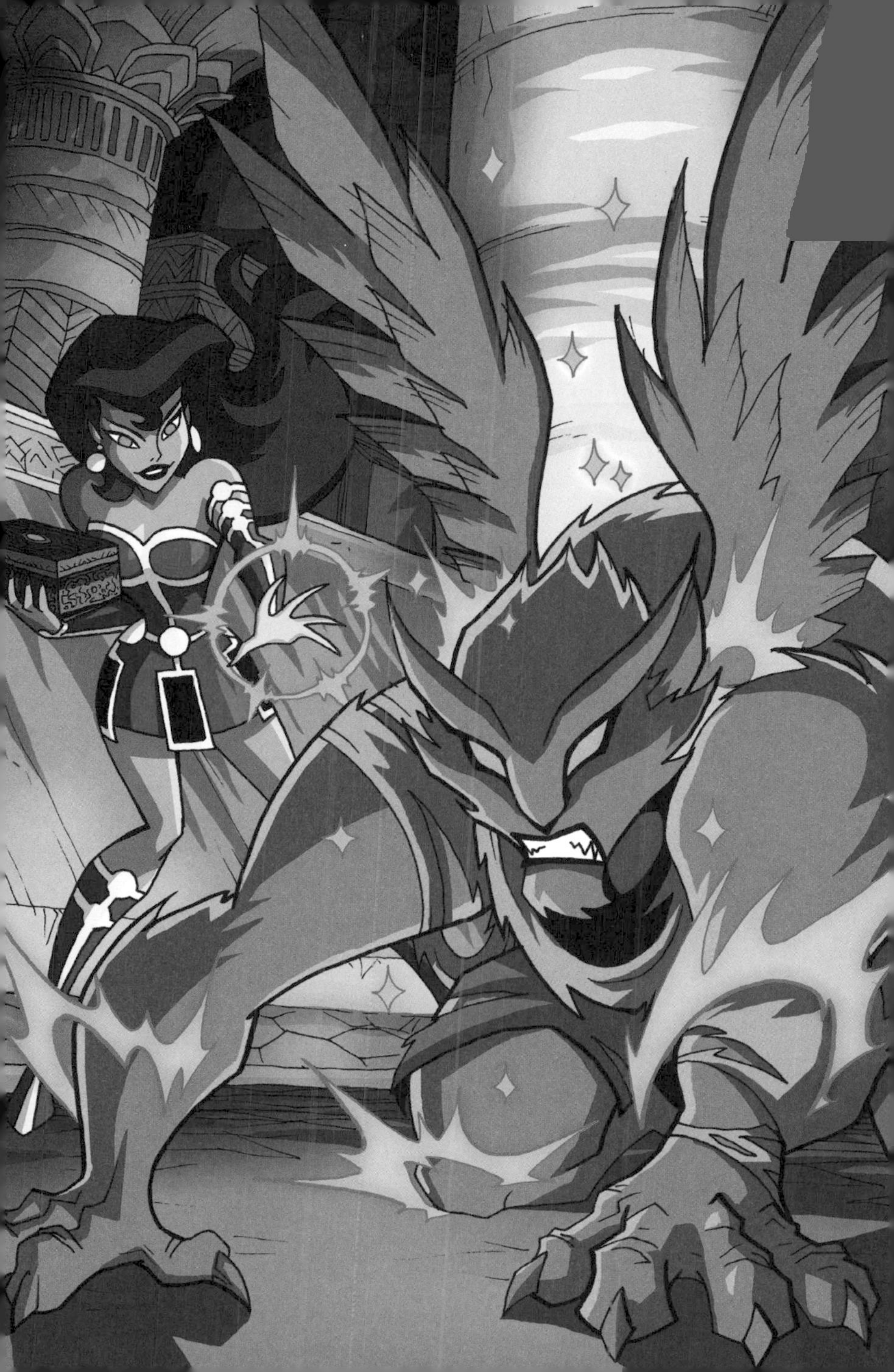

HEX MARKS THE SPOT

Circe rode on the back of her new slave. They flew above the crater of Mt. Vesuvius. Steam hissed from cracks in the rocks. The cone had collapsed in on itself after an eruption long ago. But the mountain was not dead. It was just sleeping.

"Powers of flame and fire," Circe chanted, "take me to what I desire!"

A blaze of energy shot from Circe's hand. **KA-BLAM!** It blasted a hole in the floor of the crater. A deep tunnel dropped down into the earth.

"Spell of safety I invoke," Circe said, "to form on me a protective cloak."

A shimmering bubble appeared around the sorceress and her creature. They flew into the volcano.

Smoke and steam formed a fog around them as they dropped deeper and deeper underground. Circe could smell the stink of sulphur through the protection spell.

Suddenly the tunnel got very narrow. The glowing orb of the protection spell hit the sides of the wall. Every time the globe bounced against the walls, Circe was tossed around like a bug in a jar.

"Clear my way — now, I say!"

BLAM! Another blast of energy erupted from Circe's hands. The tunnel expanded all around her.

The passage was wider now, but the magic blast had weakened the tunnel's walls. **BLOOOOSH!** Magma broke into the tunnel. The slave creature did not like that. He flapped his wings to escape. Circe slapped him on the head.

"Don't act like a chicken, or I'll turn you into one!" she said. "My spell is strong enough to protect us."

They rushed toward the magma waterfall. **SPLOOOSH!** They plunged into the lava. The slave creature was relieved to find he was still alive.

"See, scaredy cat?" the sorceress said. "There's nothing to worry about."

Then something slammed into the globe of protection. **WHAAAAAM!** A huge mouth filled with teeth tried to bite through the orb. Claws ripped at the spell.

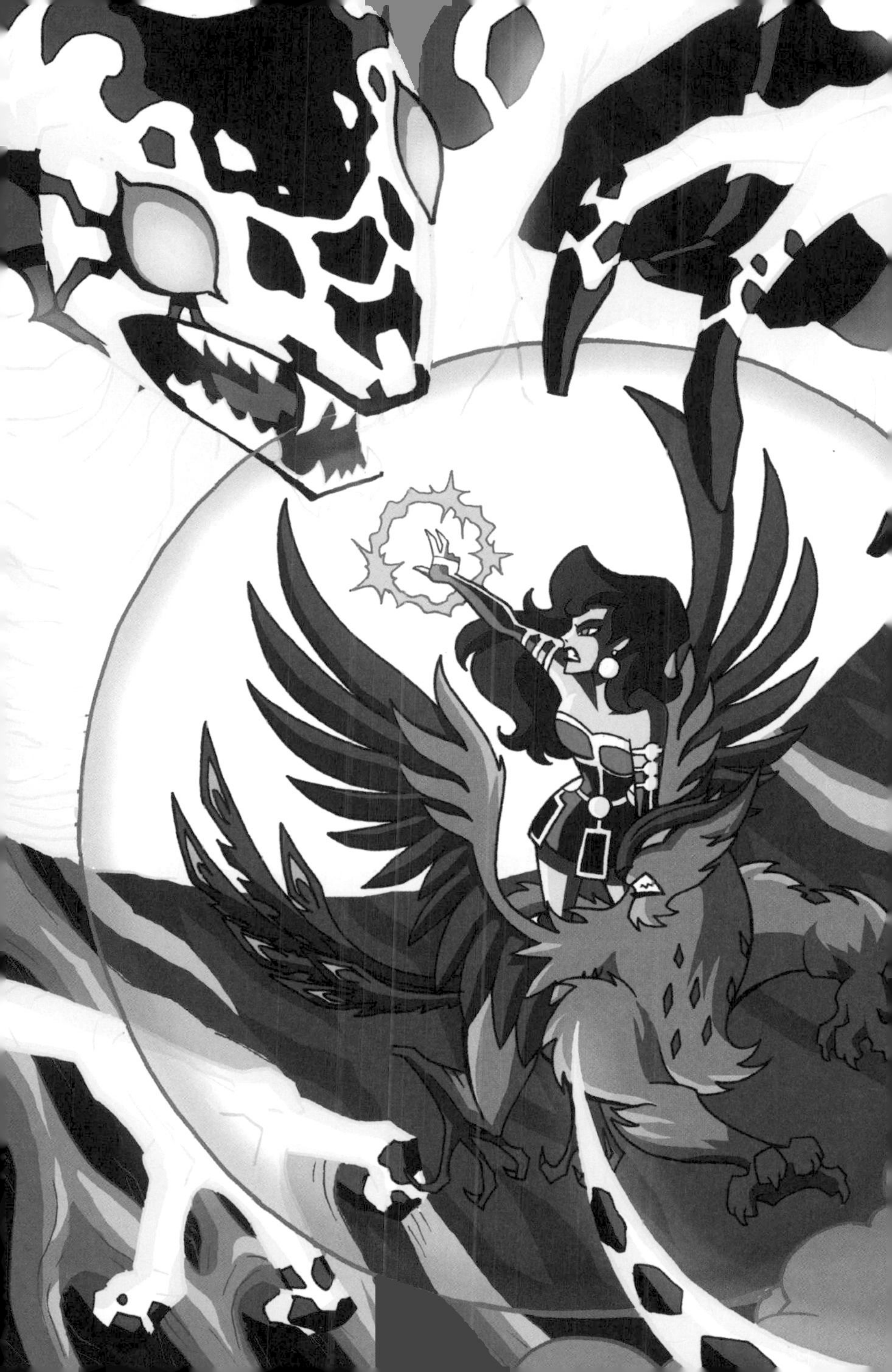

The creature chomped on the magical globe. Molten drool dripped all over the protection spell.

"A Salamander!" Circe said. She recognized the legendary and deadly fire beast. "I don't have time for this."

She pointed a finger at the beast. "Monster born of fire," Circe chanted, "it's time for you to retire!"

The Salamander yelped. It let go of the protection spell and swam away.

Circe smiled and continued her journey. The globe exited from the lava flow. The slave creature spread his wings and flew deeper into the volcano.

Soon Circe saw a spark of light in the distance. "It's a hex!" she realized. "It marks the spot of the Trinity Beast!" She reached out to touch the hex symbol.

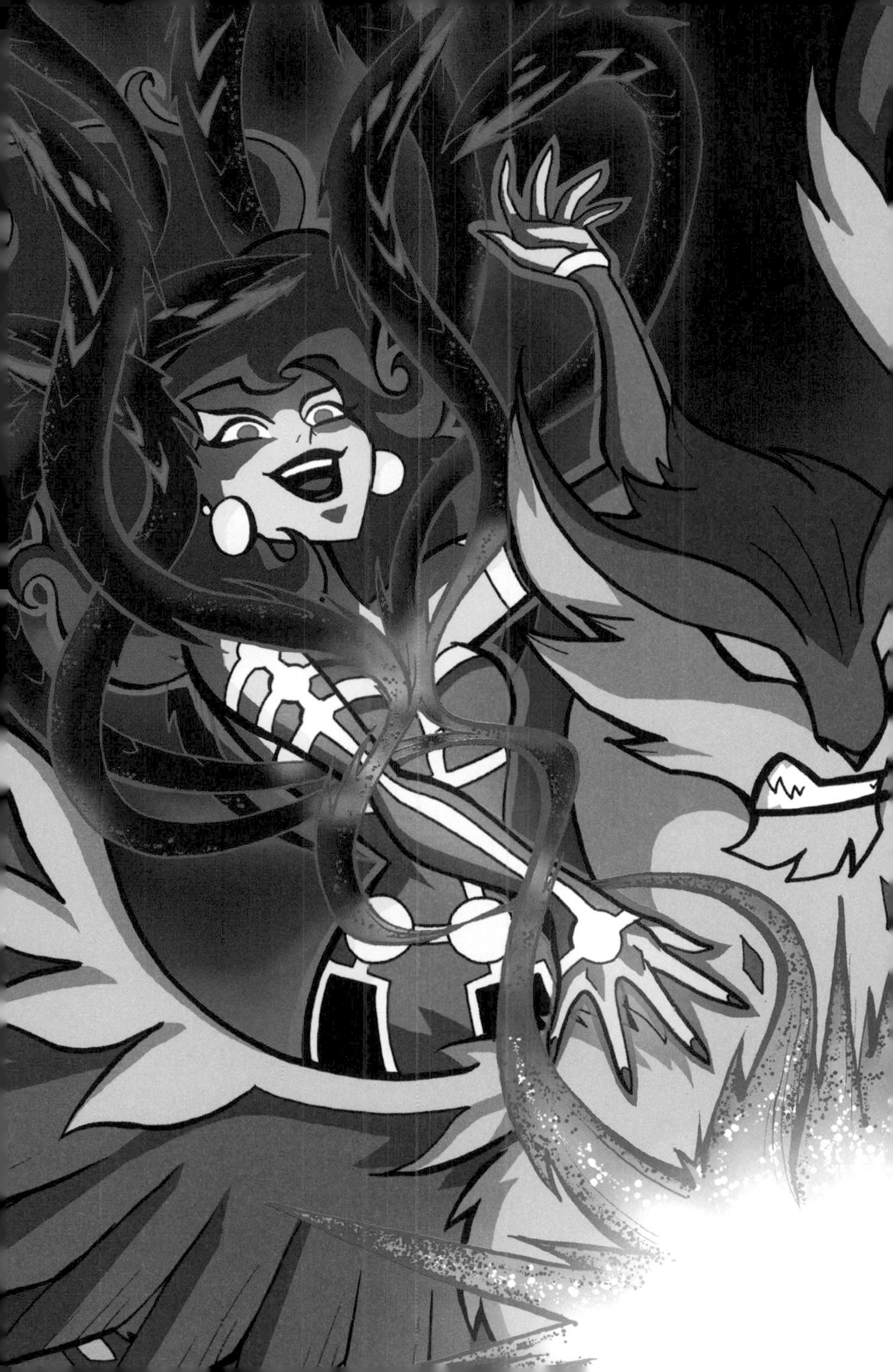

KIRRRSH! A surge of power went right through the protection spell. It rushed up her arm and into her. An aura formed around her upper body in the shape of the Hydra, a many-headed serpent.

"The power of the Hydra is mine!" Circe shouted. "Soon the Griffin and Gorgon will obey my commands too."

The sorceress could feel the other fragments calling out to her.

Circe spoke a teleportation spell. **POOOOF!** She and the slave creature were instantly transported to the sky above Mt. Vesuvius. They looked down and saw flowing lava!

Circe laughed. "Oops," she said. "It looks like my magic blasts inside the volcano have caused an eruption. Look out below, little mortals!"

The sorceress returned her creature his normal state and teleported him home. She did not need his help to find the rest of the Trinity Beast fragments.

"Hydra!" she said. "Show me the next piece of the Trinity Beast!" Circe felt a magical urge to go north. She left Vesuvius behind her, indifferent to the nearby city of Pompeii's imminent destruction.

WOOOOOOOOOSH!

Suddenly, a red, blue, and gold blur shot through the sky. Wonder Woman had arrived! She jumped out of her Invisible Jet and landed in front of the molten tidal wave.

Quickly, she used her amazing Amazon strength to dig a trench around the entire city of Pompeii. The lava gushed down the channel and away from the town.

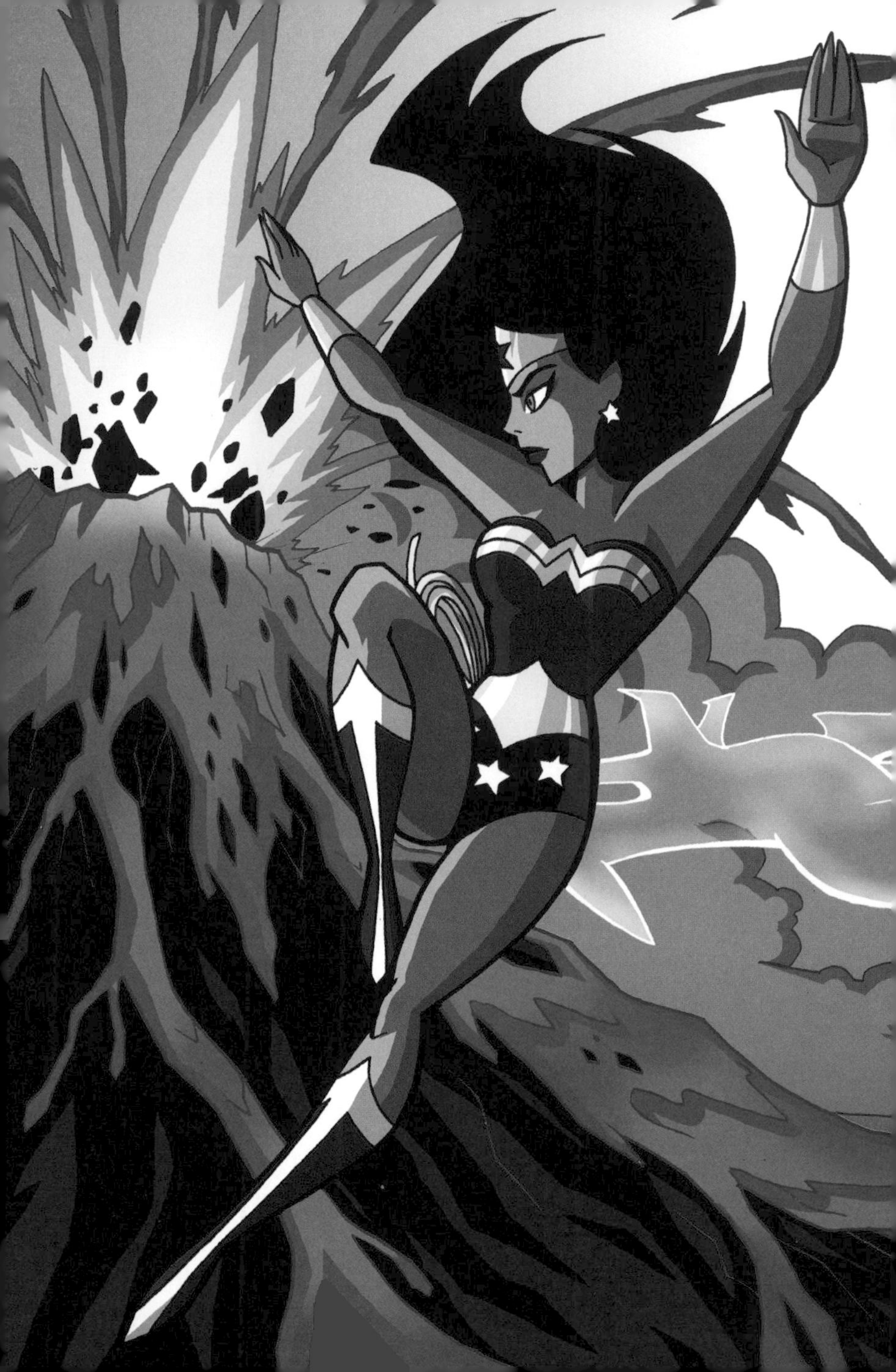

Then Wonder Woman ran at super-speed and grabbed several boulders. She threw them back into the crater of the volcano.

WHUMP! WHUMP! WHUMP!

They plugged the volcano, stopping the flow of lava.

The threat was over. But Wonder Woman had no idea that Circe was just getting started.

CHAPTER 3

HYDRA'S HEADS

Circe flew through the Arctic's snowy skies with the magical Hydra's help. Icebergs floated in the sea below her. Suddenly the ghostly image of the Hydra stretched its many heads toward a giant chunk of ice. Circe felt her eyes turn toward an iceberg. A bright hex symbol burned inside.

"Another hex marks the spot!" she said.

The sorceress landed on the giant block of polar ice. It started to vibrate the moment her feet touched the surface.

"Power of the Griffin be free!" she chanted. "Break from your prison and come to me!"

BLAAAAM! The top of the iceberg exploded. Its sides split. Huge splinters of ice fell into the ocean. SPLASH! Giant waves rose up and out from the iceberg.

The Griffin fragment of the Trinity Beast floated into Circe's open hands. The moment she touched it, she felt its awesome power. The sorceress pressed the two pieces together. CLINK!

Raw energy crawled up Circe's arms from the combined fragments of the Trinity Beast. The magic was stronger than anything the sorceress had ever experienced. It burned like fire! It made her madly happy.

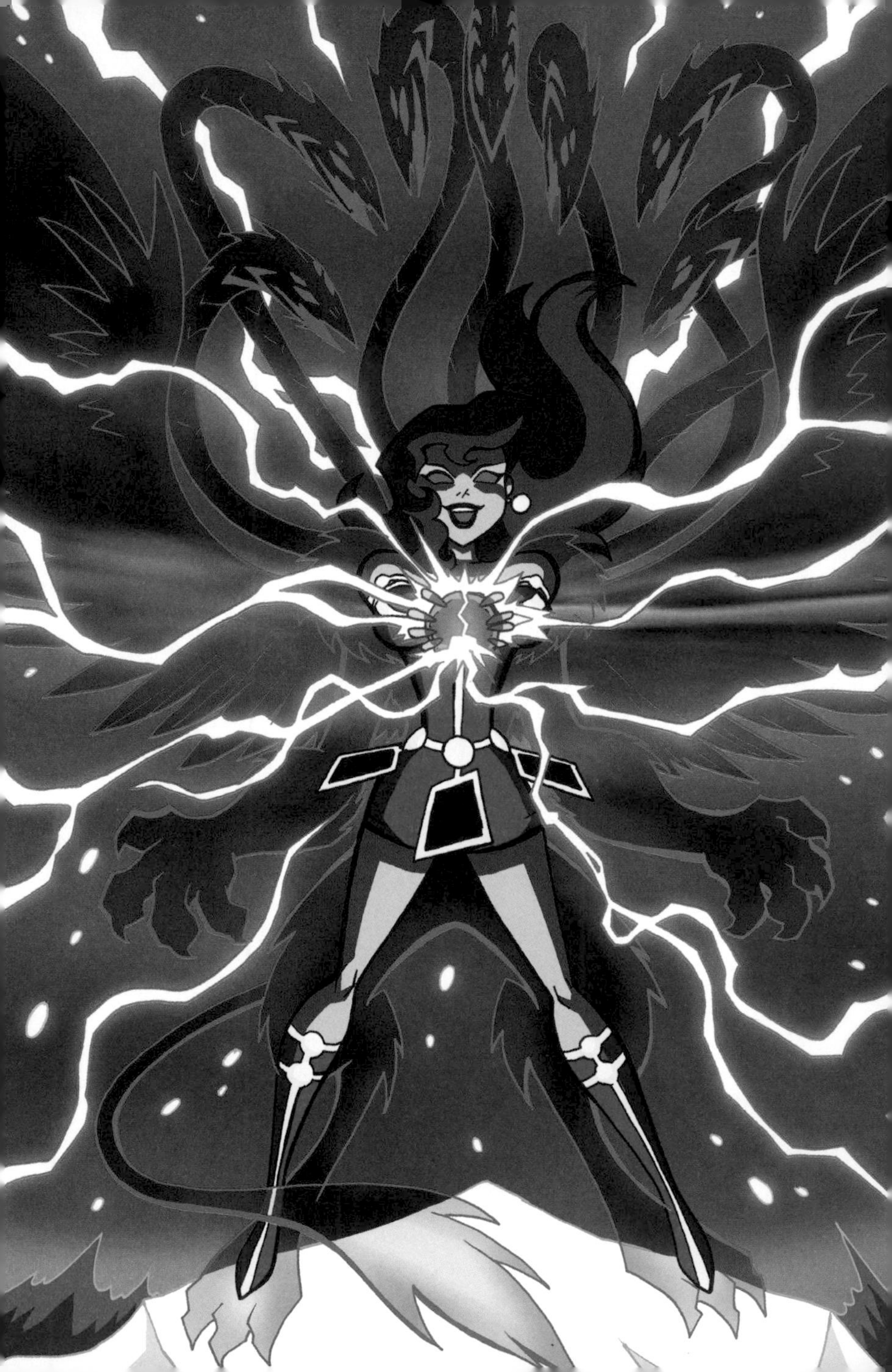

A ghostly griffin shape formed over Circe's arms, torso, and legs. It had the body of a lion and the wings of an eagle. It combined with the Hydra heads to make the silhouette of a fearsome beast.

"ROOOOOAR!" Circe bellowed. Her eyes went wide. She had not meant to growl.

Just then, the sorceress felt a pull to go south. The third fragment of the Trinity Beast was calling to her. Circe spread her Griffin wings. They were almost invisible, but they caught the air all the same. She flew high into the sky and headed south.

Circe soared over the waves from the shattered iceberg. She watched the fragments hit a nearby cargo ship, then laughed when the humans ran around in a panic on the deck.

Suddenly a bright figure in red, blue, and gold landed on the bow of the ship.

"**GRRRROAR!**" Circe growled. Her voice was a mix of her own, the Hydra's, and the Griffin's. "It's Wonder Woman!"

She did not think. Her hatred for the Amazon Princess made her act. Circe swooped down on her nemesis and slammed into her. **KA-THUMP!**

Wonder Woman fell onto the deck with a **THUD!**

"Great Hera!" the Amazon exclaimed. "What was that?"

Circe circled in the air and rushed at Wonder Woman. The Griffin wings made her blindingly fast. **WHAM!** She struck at her foe with the Griffin claws. **CHOMP!** She snapped with the Hydra jaws.

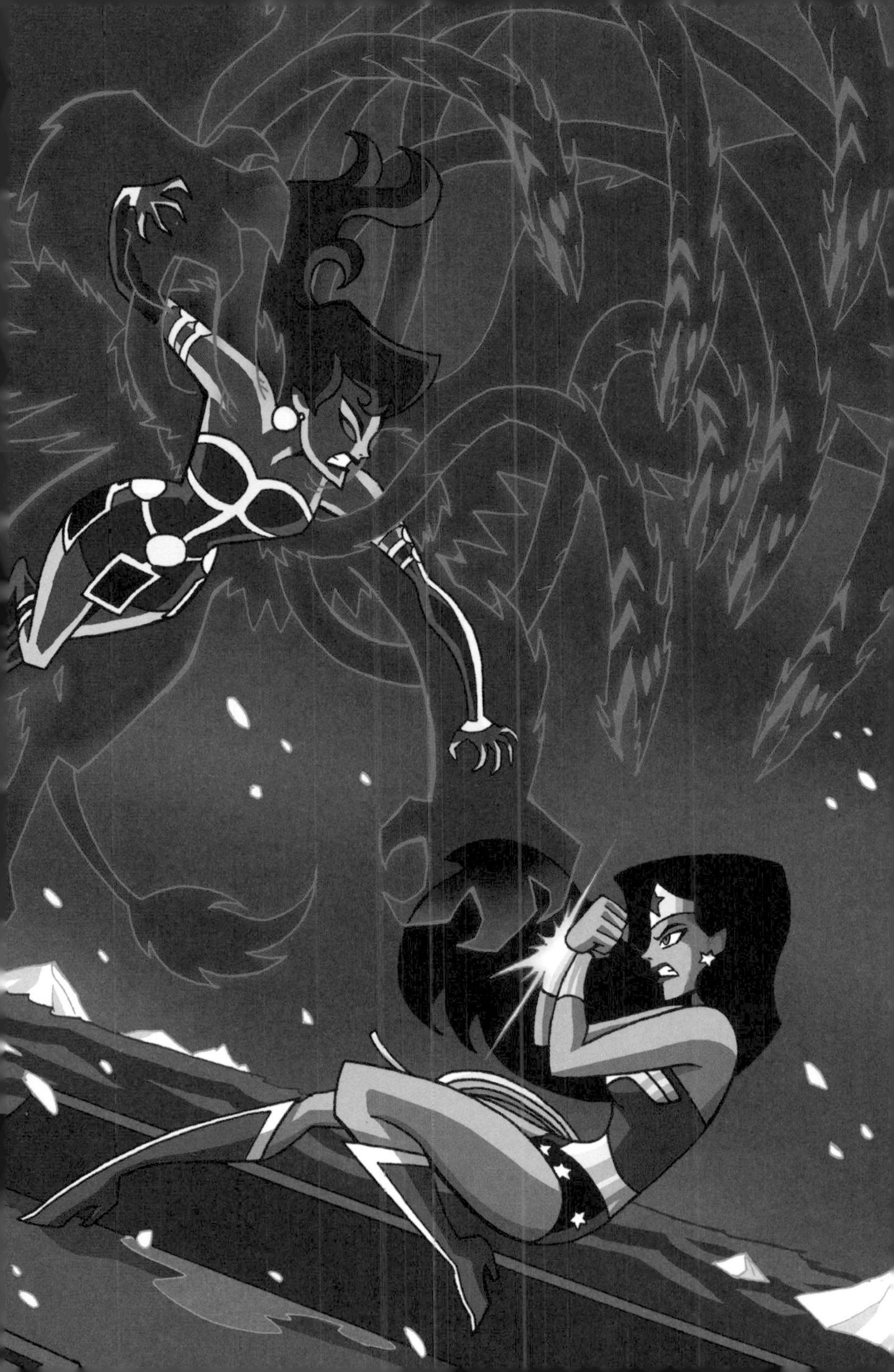

Wonder Woman defended herself with her unbreakable bracelets. *CLANG! CLANK! CLINK!* The Hydra's teeth cracked against the super-hard metal.

Up close, Wonder Woman could see Circe behind the ghastly beast. "Circe!" she said. "What has happened to you?"

"Hello, Princess," Circe said. "How do you like my new pet?" When the sorceress smiled, all of the Hydra's heads did too.

One of the heads still held Wonder Woman's wrist in its toothless jaws. Another head twisted down and grabbed the Amazon's other wrist. Then they started to pull in opposite directions. Wonder Woman could feel her muscles stretch as the Hydra heads pulled at her limbs.

Wonder Woman planted her feet on the deck of the ship and braced herself.

She used her incredible Amazon strength to pull her arms together. The two Hydra heads slammed into each other. **WHAAAM!** The heads were stunned by the blow. They let go of her limbs.

Wonder Woman jumped into the air and came down hard on the Griffin's back. **THUD!** Circe was flattened.

"Ungh," the sorceress moaned. She was dizzy from the blow. Then she felt the Griffin's wings flap. They lifted her into the air without her telling them to do so.

Circe was being carried south toward the third fragment while her archenemy was left standing on the cargo ship.

"No . . . I want to finish off . . . Wonder Woman," Circe protested. Her body felt weak, but the Griffin kept flying.

CHAPTER 4

THE GORGON FRAGMENT

The Griffin was flying the sorceress to the hiding place of the Gorgon fragment of the Trinity Beast. The Caribbean Sea was vivid blue below Circe. She could see the shallow sea bottom and small islands.

The Hydra heads all pointed in one direction. Circe could see what they saw. A small point of bright light pulsed underwater.

"The final hex!" Circe said. She urged the Griffin wings to fly faster. All she could think about was her goal to complete the Trinity Beast.

The Hydra heads stretched their necks toward the bright hex light. It was in the water right under the Griffin paws. Circe plunged into the sea. She did not speak a protection spell. She did not need one. The Hydra and Griffin shielded her.

The sorceress headed for the deepest, darkest part of the tropical sea. Huge stone blocks lay on the seabottom. They looked to be in ruins, but Circe knew they were part of a building. The hex light burned like an underwater fire within the debris. Circe had to get to it!

"Stones come apart! Show me the hex," she said, "and what comes next!"

Raw energy beams shot from Circe's Griffin paws. The ancient stone blocks exploded. BUBBLE! BUBBLE! The sea turned into wild foam all around her.

Sand and silt made thick clouds in the water. Circe could not see anything. So she commanded the Hydra heads to wiggle like snakes into the sand. She used the Griffin paws to dig through the scattered ancient blocks.

WOOOSH! She swam into the ruins to find a huge room filled with statues. In the hands of the third statue, in the middle of the room, was the hex light — and it surrounded the final fragment!

Circe reached out to touch the Gorgon fragment. **FWOOOOSH!** A colorful, dancing light settled around the third statue. Its appearance changed from stone to a silhouette.

"You have freed me!" the fragment said, its light pulsating as it spoke. "Now we will become one . . ."

FAZIRRRRT! More magical energy exploded outward. Circe's body blazed with light. The Hydra and Griffin howled like wild beasts. Their unleashed fury surged through Circe's body.

Suddenly, all three fragments of the Trinity Beast floated above Circe like a crown.

BOOOOOOOOOM! Hydra, Griffin, and Gorgon combined. The three monsters of myth became one. The Griffin's lion tail changed into a snake. Its head became the face of a woman with serpents for hair. This was Medusa, the most dangerous Gorgon in all mythology. Her gaze turned human flesh to stone.

The completed form of the Trinity Beast surrounded Circe. She was enveloped with the creature's glow.

Now Circe had the power to destroy her hated enemy once and for all! But something felt . . . wrong.

The ghastly image of the Trinity Beast around Circe solidified. Suddenly, she was trapped inside the monster. She had no control over her own body. She was completely helpless.

Circe screamed.

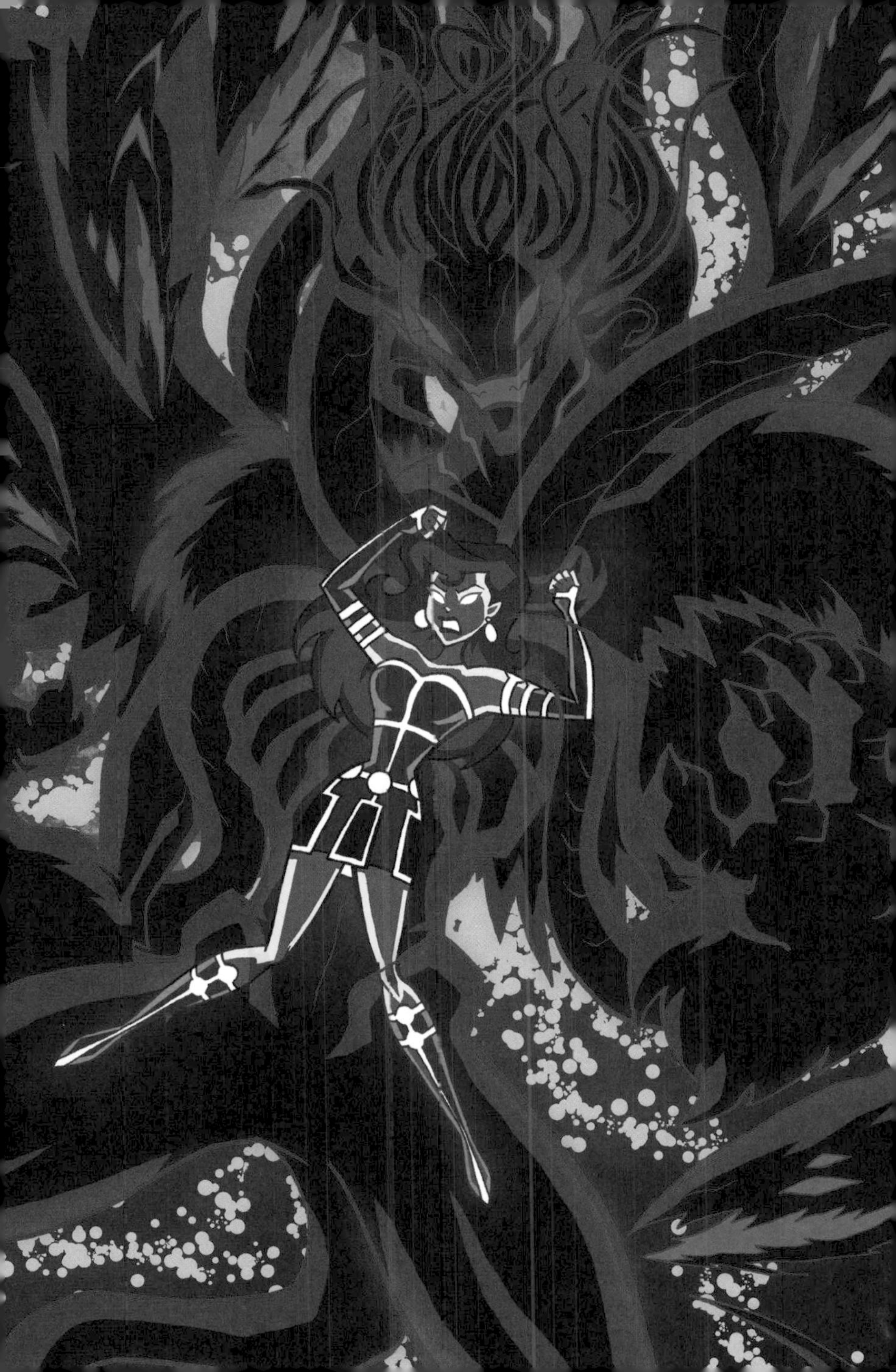

OUT OF CONTROL

WHAAAAAM! The Trinity Beast burst out from the ancient ruins. It headed for the surface of the sea.

Circe had no idea what the monster was doing. It was beyond her control. The Trinity Beast was using Circe for its own purposes.

"Beast of old," she said, "I regain my hold!"

But Circe's spell didn't work on the Trinity Beast.

This is why the Trinity Beast was broken into fragments and hidden so long ago, she realized. *No one can control this creature!*

SPLASH! The Trinity Beast burst out from the water. Its wings shook themselves dry, and it soared above the sea. In the distance were the sparkling skyscrapers of Miami, Florida. The Trinity Beast turned toward them.

The people of Miami were used to dangers like hurricanes, floods, and even a super-villain now and then. They were not ready to face the Trinity Beast. The monster swooped along the streets of downtown.

SCREEEEECH! Cars skidded.

"HELP!" People screamed.

WOOOOP WOOOP! Police sirens blared.

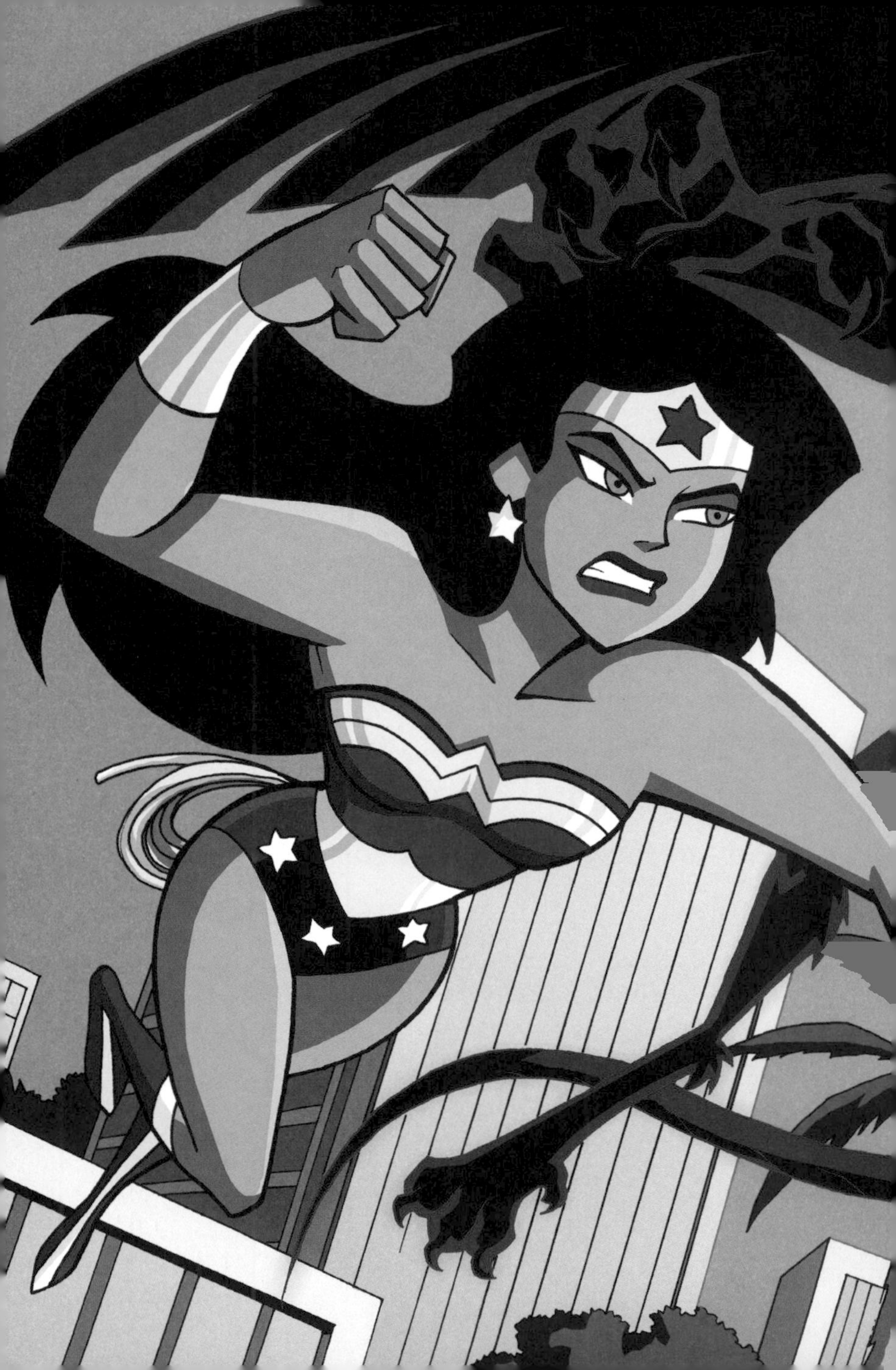

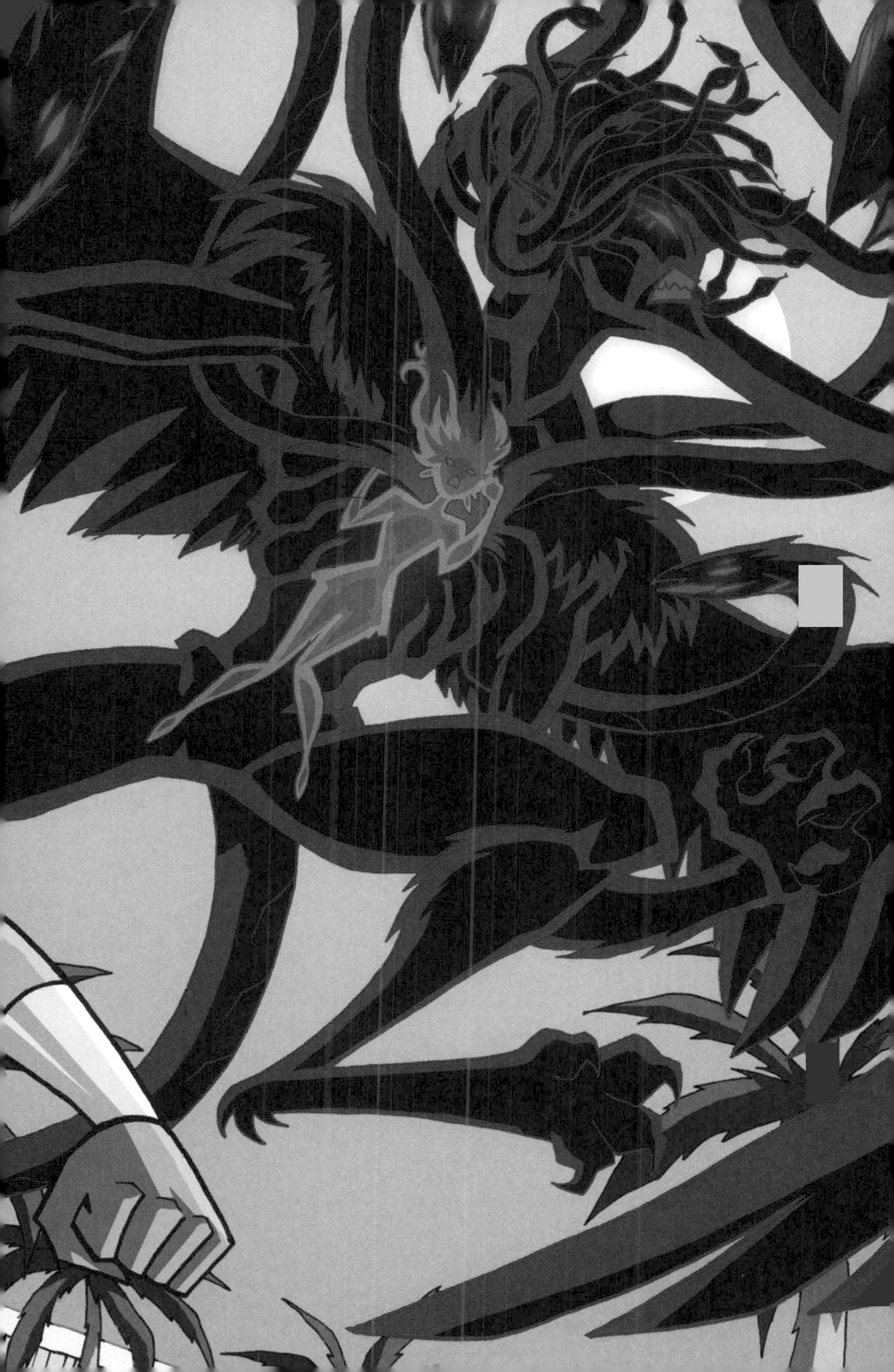

Suddenly a figure in red, blue, and gold slammed into the Trinity Beast.

WHAAAAAM! The monster was knocked all the way back to the beach. **WHOMMMP!** It landed on its back in the sand. **OOOOF!** Circe had the breath knocked out of her.

Wonder Woman landed nearby. The sight of her archenemy filled Circe with wild rage.

ROOARRR! The monster snapped at Wonder Woman with its multiple jaws. The Amazing Amazon blocked the attack with her bracelets.

CLAAAANG! CRAAAACK! The monster's teeth shattered.

"Don't you ever learn?" Wonder Woman said.

FWA-SLASH! The Griffin's tail cracked like a whip. Wonder Woman easily dodged it.

ZIRRRT! The Medusa head glared at the Amazon Princess, trying to turn her to stone. Wonder Woman used her golden tiara as a mirror to watch the Beast's movements. As long as she did not look directly into Medusa's eyes, she was safe from the monster's curse.

Circe could not think. She was filled with primitive fury. The only thought in her head was to destroy her enemy. **WHAAAAAM!** A super-punch to the Hydra head snapped her out of her rage-induced haze. Now she was filled with fear instead.

The Trinity Beast is taking over my mind! she realized in horror. *I'm forgetting who I am!*

The sorceress clawed at her prison, desperate to escape. The Griffin paws waved wildly in the air. The Trinity Beast lost focus for a moment.

Wonder Woman saw her chance. The Amazon put all her mighty strength behind a power punch.

KAPOWWWW! The Beast was smashed into the sand.

The Beast became transparent again, showing Circe inside.

Suddenly, a brilliant golden light passed before Circe's eyes. Her skin started to tingle. She could feel the Beast's energy leaving her. Finally, the golden light wrapped around the Trinity Beast's form and pulled it out and away from Circe's body.

FWOOOOOFFF!

Just like that, the monster vanished into thin air. Circe fell into the sand and lay on her back for a few moments.

Circe was struggling to figure out what had happened. Then she saw Wonder Woman hovering above her, holding her in the loop of her Golden Lasso. Circe knew that within the grasp of the brilliant rope, illusions and magic were instantly dispelled.

The sorceress watched Wonder Woman smash the Beast's fragments between her bracelets. CRUNCH! It was broken into tiny pieces, and so was the spell of the Trinity Beast. Wonder Woman threw the remaining pieces as far as she could. The useless pieces of stone disappeared from sight and landed somewhere in the ocean.

Circe felt the Golden Lasso wrap around her body. **WHOOOSH! WOOSH! WOOSH!**

Caught in the lasso's grasp, Circe could not move a muscle. Once more, she was trapped.

"Not again," Circe said.

Circe's hatred boiled inside her. Being trapped inside the Golden Lasso was far, far worse than being trapped inside the Trinity Beast.

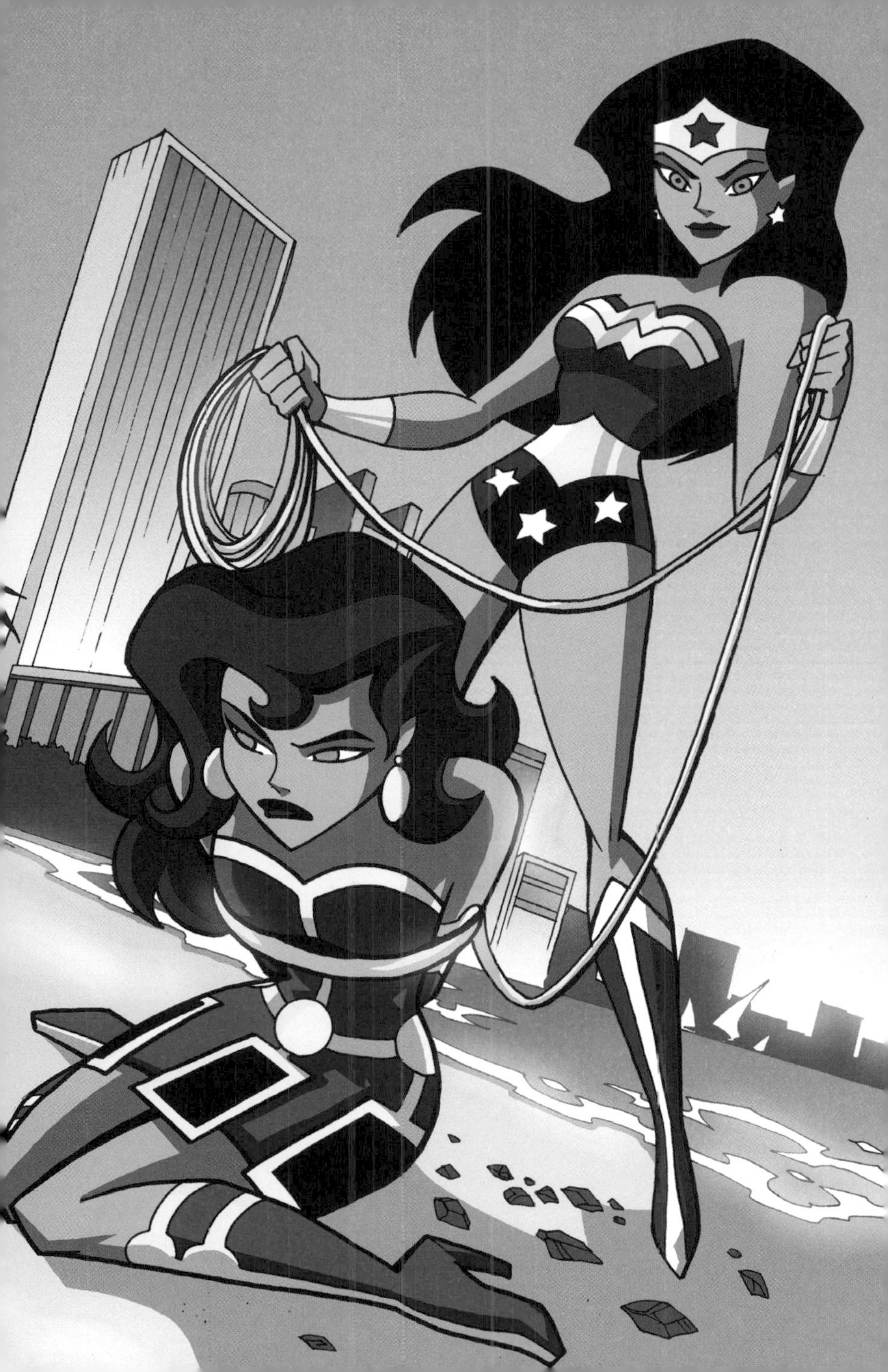

SUPER HEROES VS.

SUPER DC HEROES
THE DARK KNIGHT
BATMAN VS THE CAT COMMANDER

BATMAN VS. THE CAT COMMANDER

SUPER DC HEROES
THE MAN OF STEEL
SUPERMAN AND THE POISONED PLANET

SUPERMAN AND THE POISONED PLANET

SUPER DC HEROES
The FLASH
KILLER KALEIDOSCOPE

THE FLASH: KILLER KALEIDOSCOPE

SUPER DC HEROES
AQUAMAN
DEEPWATER DISASTER

AQUAMAN: DEEPWATER DISASTER

SUPER DC HEROES
GREEN LANTERN
GUARDIAN OF EARTH

GREEN LANTERN: GUARDIAN OF EARTH

SUPER DC HEROES
WONDER WOMAN
TRIAL OF THE AMAZONS

WONDER WOMAN: TRIAL OF THE AMAZONS

WHICH SIDE...

SUPER-VILLAINS

JOKER
ON THE
HIGH SEAS

JOKER ON THE HIGH SEAS

LEX LUTHOR
AND THE
KRYPTONITE CAVERNS

LEX LUTHOR AND THE KRYPTONITE CAVERNS

CAPTAIN COLD
AND THE
BLIZZARD BATTLE

CAPTAIN COLD AND THE BLIZZARD BATTLE

BLACK MANTA
AND THE
OCTOPUS ARMY

BLACK MANTA AND THE OCTOPUS ARMY

SINESTRO
AND THE
RING OF FEAR

SINESTRO AND THE RING OF FEAR

CHEETAH
AND THE
PURRFECT CRIME

CHEETAH AND THE PURRFECT CRIME

WILL YOU CHOOSE?

IF YOU WERE WONDER WOMAN

Anyone caught in Wonder Woman's Golden Lasso must tell the truth. If you were Wonder Woman, what questions would you ask Circe to make her incriminate herself?

Wonder Woman owns a pair of indestructible bracelets. What are some ways Wonder Woman could use her bracelets in battle?

IF YOU WERE CIRCE

Circe seeks to attain a great power, but ultimately the power takes control of her. Look through the text for hints that the Trinity Beast might be more dangerous than Circe thinks.

Circe has the ability to turn anyone into a servant creature. What kind of servant creature would you create if you had Circe's powers?

AUTHOR BIO

Laurie Sutton has read comics since she was a kid. She grew up to become an editor for Marvel, DC Comics, Starblaze, and Tekno Comics. She has written Adam Strange for DC, Star Trek: Voyager for Marvel, plus Star Trek: Deep Space Nine and Witch Hunter for Malibu Comics. There are long boxes of comics in her closet where there should be clothing and shoes. Laurie has lived all over the world. She currently resides in Florida.

SUPER HERO GLOSSARY

Invisible Jet (in-VIZ-uh-buhl JET)—Wonder Woman sometimes uses her Invisible Jet to reach places that require fast, airborne travel

invulnerable (in-VUHL-ner-uh-buhl)—as an Amazon warrior, Wonder Woman is invulnerable, or immune to harm

Golden Lasso (GOHL-den LASS-oh)—the Golden Lasso, or Lasso of Truth, forces anyone caught in its grasp to tell the truth. It also dispels magic and illusions.

super-speed—Wonder Woman can run, dodge, and jump extremely fast

super-strength—Wonder Woman is incredibly strong

ILLUSTRATOR BIO

Luciano Vecchio was born in 1982 and currently lives in Buenos Aires, Argentina. With experience in illustration, animation, and comics, his works have been published in the US, Spain, UK, France, and Argentina. His credits include Ben 10 (DC Comics), Cruel Thing (Norma), Unseen Tribe (Zuda Comics), and Sentinels (Drumfish Productions).

SUPER-VILLAIN GLOSSARY

chaos (KAY-oss)—total confusion. Circe loves creating chaos with her spells while battling Wonder Woman.

curse (KURSS)—an evil spell intended to do harm. Circe can cast curses on her enemies.

hex (HEKS)—a spell or charm that prevents others from accessing something, like the hex on the Hydra fragment.

immortal (i-MOHR-tuhl)—living or lasting forever

nemesis (NEM-uh-sis)—a longstanding opponent. Circe is Wonder Woman's nemesis.

Pandora's Box (pan-DOR-uhz BOKS)—according to myth, an ancient Greek artifact that contained all the evil in the world. The Trinity Beast was once imprisoned in Pandora's Box.

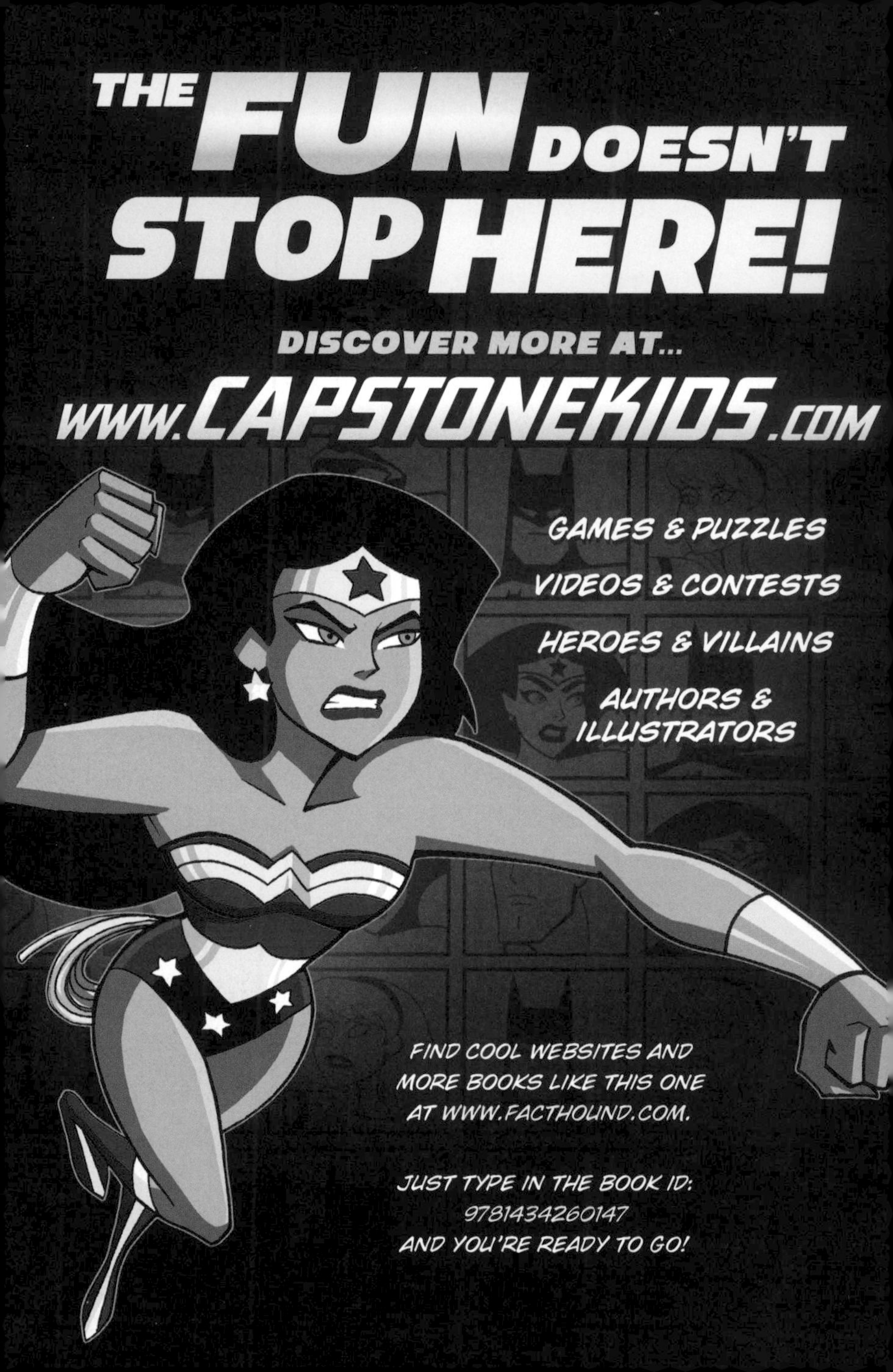

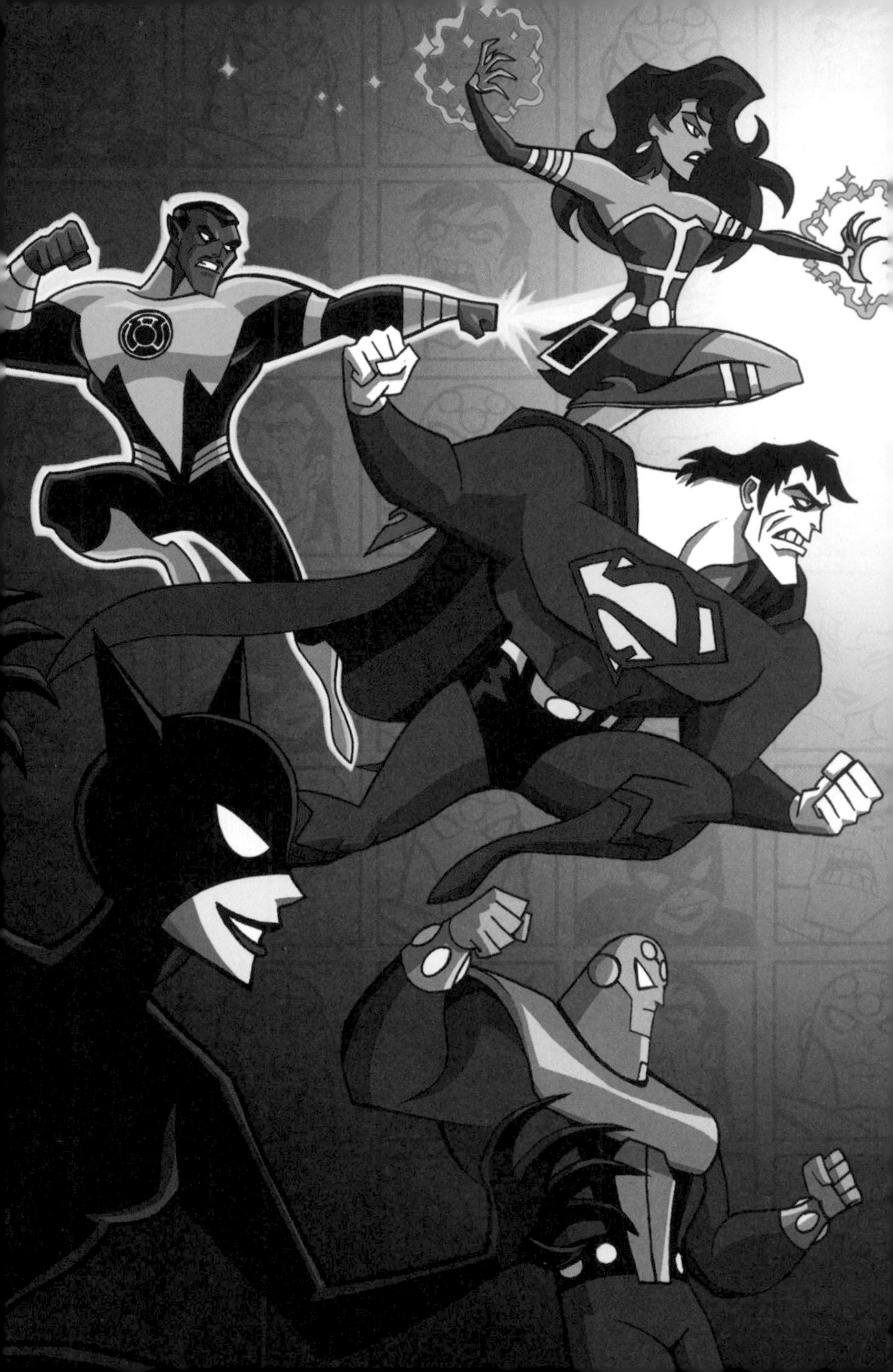